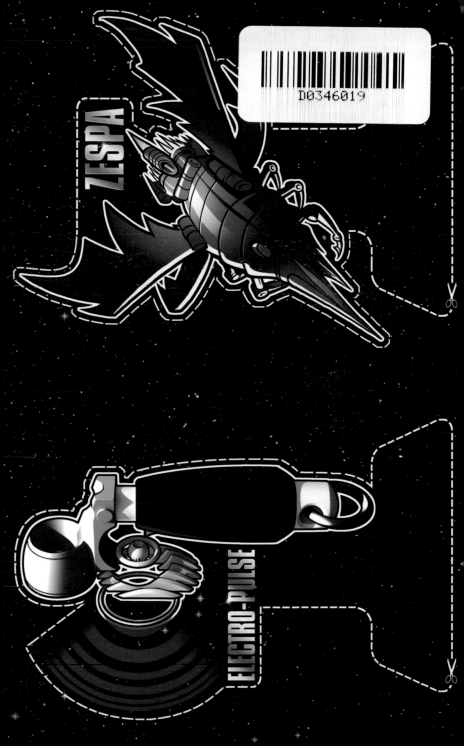

ZESPA

ELECTRO-PULSE

D0346019

Status: Used by smugglers to defend Haven
Species: Wasp-bot
Galaxy: Milky Way
Traits: Wasp-like robots with sharp blades, fly in swarms

Status: Hand-held electro-magnetic device
Species: Made by humans
Galaxy: Milky Way
Traits: Disables computers and circuitry

To my wonderful Jackie

Special thanks to Benjamin Scott

Bloomsbury Publishing, London, New Delhi, New York and Sydney

First published in Great Britain in August 2012 by Bloomsbury Publishing Plc
50 Bedford Square, London, WC1B 3DP

A CIP catalogue record for this book is available from the British Library

ISBN 978 1 4088 2715 4

Typeset by Hewer Text UK Ltd, Edinburgh
Printed in Great Britain by Clays Ltd, St Ives plc, Bungay, Suffolk

1 3 5 7 9 10 8 6 4 2

www.bloomsbury.com
www.starfighterbooks.com

MAX CHASE

Illustrated by Sam Hadley

BLOOMSBURY

LONDON NEW DELHI NEW YORK SYDNEY

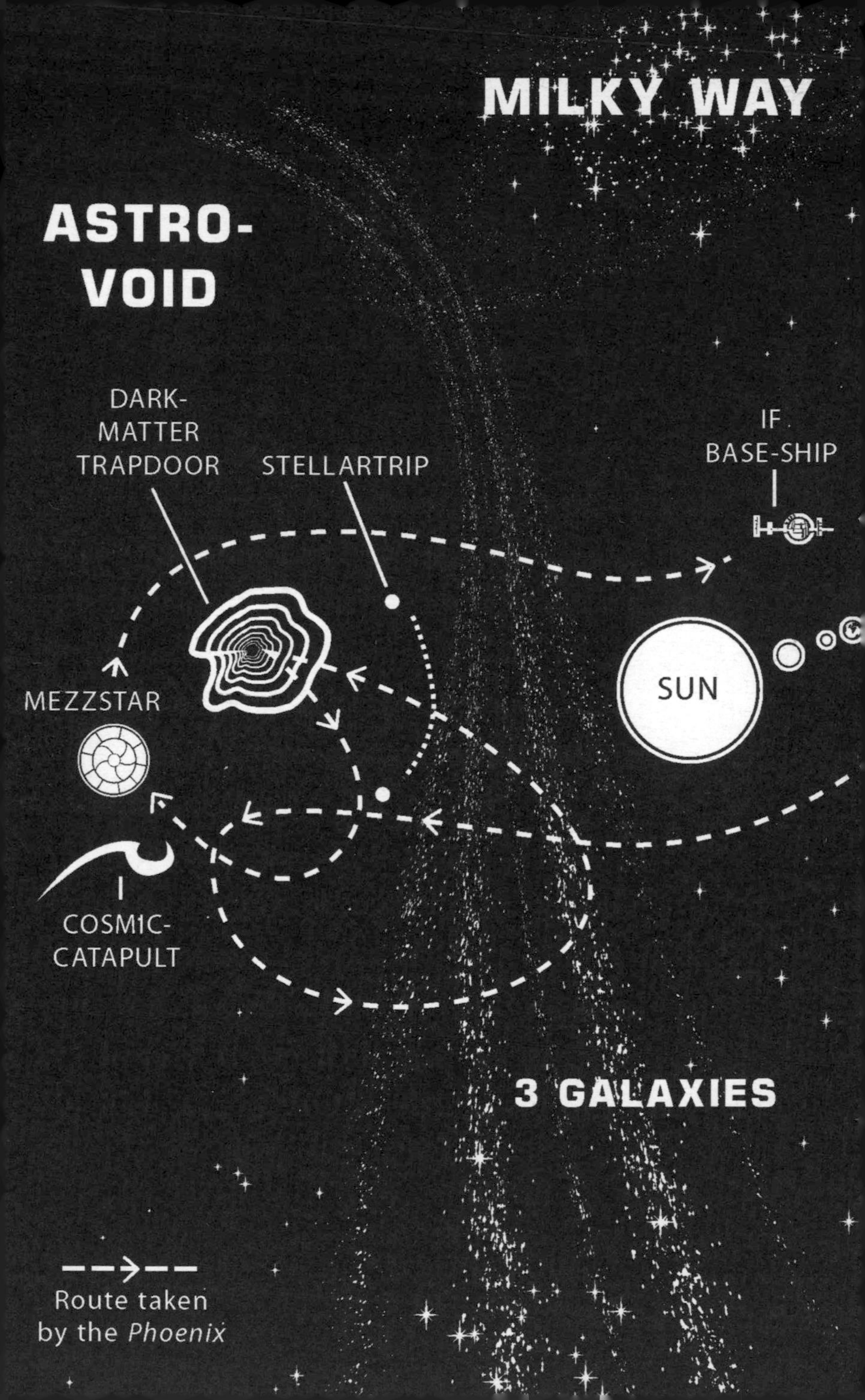
MILKY WAY
ASTRO-VOID
DARK-MATTER TRAPDOOR
STELLARTRIP
IF BASE-SHIP
MEZZSTAR
SUN
COSMIC-CATAPULT
3 GALAXIES
Route taken by the *Phoenix*

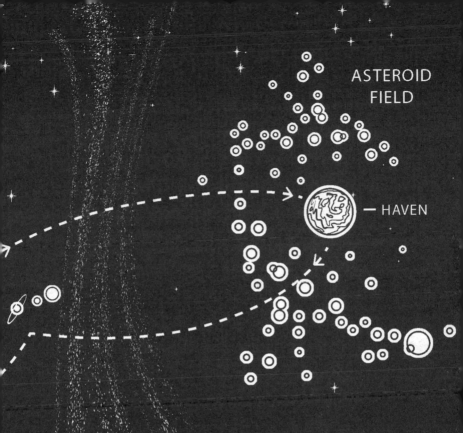

ASTEROID
FIELD

— HAVEN

RUMANA
GALAXY

7 GALAXIES

STAR FIGHTERS

An elite fighting team sworn to protect and defend the galaxy

It is the year 5012 and the Milky Way galaxy is under attack . . .

After the Universal War . . . a war that almost brought about the destruction of every known universe . . . the planets in the Milky Way banded together to create the Intergalactic Force – an elite fighting team sworn to protect and defend the galaxy.

Only the brightest and most promising students are accepted into the Intergalactic Force Academy, and only the very best cadets reach the highest of their ranks and become . . .

To be a Star Fighter is to dedicate your life to one mission: *Peace in Space*. They are given the coolest weapons, the fastest spaceships – and the most dangerous missions. Everyone at the Intergalactic Force Academy wants to be a Star Fighter someday.

Do YOU have what it takes?

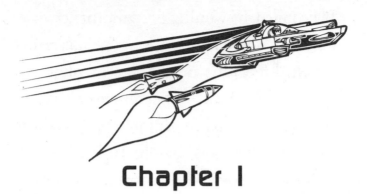

Chapter 1

'There's no hiding from me!' Peri flew his fighter pod tight around the curved hull of a star cruiser. His search beam flicked across the battered surface of the ship, looking for the next beacon.

Peri glanced at the countdown monitor. Only twenty minutes left. This was his final Star Fighter test – an obstacle course through the Milky Way. He had to collect the last three beacons and make it back to base before the clock timed out. If he succeeded, he would become the youngest ever Star Fighter.

If he failed, he wouldn't get another chance.

Peri flew over a large gash in the star cruiser's hull. He didn't need the searchlight to see the flashing beacon in a tangle of twisted metal. He plunged his fighter pod towards it. The beacon was barely bigger than a grenade. He activated the transporter beam. There was a flash of light. *'Beacon on board!'* the ship's computer announced.

'Eighteen down!' Peri whooped as he blasted away from the cruiser. 'Two to go!'

'Collision alert!' his ship screeched as warning lights flashed. Peri's heart pounded like a pulsar.

Diesel's fighter pod buzzed past.

'Diesel!' Peri yelled into the radio. He yanked the nav-stick hard, sending his tiny one-man fighter spiralling out of control.

'Having problems, wastoid? I've nearly finished.'

Wrestling with the stabilising thrusters, Peri checked the scores on the monitor. He groaned. Diesel had already collected nineteen of his twenty beacons.

'Last one to finish is a bugonaut!' Diesel radioed.

Diesel's fighter careered off to pick up his final beacon.

Peri found the next beacon on his radar. It was on the dark side of the moon. Two attack drones blasted towards him. He knew it was part of the test, but he still felt a tingle down his spine.

Peri swerved as missiles soared past, then changed direction back towards his ship.

'Heat-seekers!' Peri gasped, fumbling for the right button. If he'd been on the *Phoenix*, his bionic connection with the ship would have instantly located the deflecto-flares.

But the missiles were gaining on him. He didn't have time to find the flares.

Peri roared towards the attack drones, firing his lasers. He knew the drones had invincible armour-plating, but he had an idea that might just get him out of this mess. If he fired his lasers at their armour and made it glow plasma-hot, maybe the heat-seeking missiles would have a new target!

Peri shut off his engines and coasted towards the beacon.

The heat-seeking missiles raced for the hottest thing around – the attack drones!

KA-BLAAAM! The explosion lit up Peri's cockpit. The drones were space dust!

Peri punched the air, then steered his fighter smoothly towards the beacon. He activated the laser net. A web of laser beams curled around the flashing beacon and pulled it on board.

He checked the radar. The last beacon was near the finish line and there were just under five minutes to cross it!

He blasted around the moon and straight into the path of . . .

'Asteroids!' he yelled as he swung his way through the giant tumbling rocks. Diesel's fighter pod was right in the middle of the asteroid storm.

'I hate *prrrip'chiq* asteroids!' Diesel snapped.

'You can't shoot yourself out of this one,' Peri shouted. 'You'll create too much debris.'

'Just watch me, dumboid!' Diesel yelled.

'Don't say I didn't warn you,' Peri said, weaving through the maze of space-rocks.

He twisted and dodged until he glimpsed the narrow green laser beam of the finish line. His circuits buzzed with excitement. He was going to finish first!

Peri hit his booster rockets and darted forward.

'Peri, you must collect the last beacon before you cross the finish line.' General Pegg's voice crackled over the radio.

Aaaaaargh! How could Peri have forgotten the last beacon?

If he failed this test, someone else would take his place on the *Phoenix*. He couldn't let that happen. It wasn't just that Peri wanted else to be a Star Fighter more than anything in the solar system. He and Diesel were keeping a big secret. They had two unofficial crew members hiding on the *Phoenix*: Selene, their fearless engineer, who had been a stowaway, and Otto, a bounty hunter from planet Meigwor. If anyone found out about either of them, Peri feared he and Diesel would be kicked out of the IFA.

The final beacon was only seconds away from the finish line. Peri was going too fast for the transporter beam. He punched in the coordinates of the beacon and activated the laser net.

'*Negative,*' the computer responded. '*Too dangerous to use laser net at this speed.*'

'Override safety protocols,' Peri commanded, pressing his palm against the control panel to override the ship's computer.

'*Override accepted.*' The computer dropped the laser net in place.

Peri guided his pod towards the beacon. Blood pounded in his head. He fought hard to keep the nav-stick steady. He had one chance to get it right.

'Now,' he yelled and pulled up. As the net scooped up the beacon and brought it on board, the nav-stick was wrenched from Peri's hand. The laser net's split-second

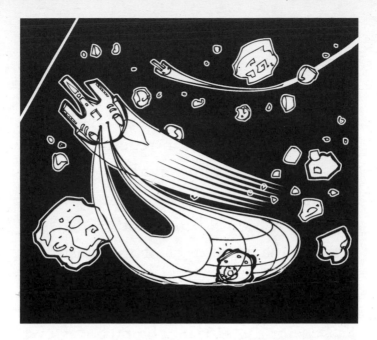

grab was like slamming on the brakes at top speed. He was thrown against the astro-harness. His fighter pod spun violently. He banged on the stabilising thrusters, but he just kept spinning.

'*S'fâh*, Peri!' Diesel yelled over the radio. 'What are you doing?' Diesel was zigzagging madly, trying to keep his own fighter pod out of Peri's way.

The finish line was just ahead. Peri slammed on the boosters. It wasn't going to be pretty, but maybe he could still do it. With the right touch, he could nudge his out-of-control fighter pod in the right direction. He punched the nav-stick left, then right. He held his breath as he spun through the green light of the finish line. He regained control just in time to see Diesel's pod cross the line. The final scores flashed on the screen. The race was over. Peri had crossed the finish line first!

'Rocket-tastic!' Peri cried. 'Eat my two point three seconds, Diesel!'

General Pegg's voice came over the radio. 'Peri and Diesel! Back to base immediately!'

Peri steered towards the IFA base-ship. General Pegg sounded really angry, but why? Peri and Diesel had both passed the final Star Fighter test.

The automatic docking controls guided the fighter pods into the landing bay. Peri's pod touched down with a jolt. He tore off the astro-harness and climbed out. Diesel stormed towards him. His narrow band of spiky hair had turned scarlet and his eyes flashed yellow.

'You cheating lamizoid!' Diesel shouted.

Before Peri could reply, General Pegg marched into the landing bay.

'I've never seen such reckless flying!' he yelled. 'I should discharge you both for endangering each other's lives!'

Peri's circuits went cold.

Had he just thrown away his chance of becoming a fully fledged Star Fighter?

Chapter 2

General Pegg flicked a finger across the touch screen of his wrist-computer and the scores on the board above the landing bay changed. 'Peri, I'm penalising you fifteen seconds.'

That's not fair, Peri wanted to shout. *I crossed the line first!*

'I win!' Diesel cheered as his band of hair turned orange in celebration.

'Be quiet, Diesel!' General Pegg yelled. 'You may have won the race – but I'm not sure either of you is mature enough to become a Star Fighter.'

Peri felt his stomach turn as if he was doing somersaults around a black hole. Diesel's hair had turned a sickly green. After a week of the most intensive training in the history of the IFA, General Pegg couldn't fail them now, could he?

One of the trainers ran over to Peri. 'You've broken the all-time record!' he said, but an angry look from General Pegg sent the trainer scurrying away.

'Using the laser net at that speed was a reckless stunt, but —' The general's mouth twitched into what could have been a smile. 'I can't fault your skill as a pilot, Peri — nor yours as a gunner, Diesel.'

The general's mouth tightened. Peri wondered what he was going to say next. 'You are young and I'm worried that you both take too many risks,' he continued, shaking his head. 'I need some time to decide if you're truly ready to become Star Fighters.'

General Pegg turned and marched from the landing bay, leaving Peri and Diesel staring at each other.

'He can't stop us becoming Star Fighters *now*, can he?' Diesel gasped.

'He can do what he wants,' Peri replied and headed for a service hatch at the edge of the landing bay.

Diesel followed him. 'Where are you going?'

'Keep your voice down,' Peri hissed. 'I'm going to the *Phoenix*.'

He climbed into one of the service tunnels that ran through the IF base-ship. 'I want to check on Selene and Otto,' he said, 'but I need to sneak on board. We don't want anyone asking too many questions. If Pegg finds out about Selene and

Otto, he won't just fail us, he'll vaporise us!'

'I can understand why Otto's hiding,' Diesel said. 'Who wants a smelly Meigwor bounty hunter around? But Selene's dad works for the IF, so why does she need to hide?'

'There has to be a reason she stowed away on the *Phoenix* in the first place. She'll tell us when she's ready.' Peri pushed past a stack of crates, then held up a hand to stop Diesel. 'There's a camera at the corner,' he said. 'We need to stick close against this wall. It's in the camera's blind spot. I've memorised a sensor-free route from the blueprints. We'll still need to be really careful though.'

Peri and Diesel shuffled along, then slipped through a door into a main corridor. At the end of the corridor was an

entrance portal that lead to the launch bay. After activating the doors they hid at the sides and peered round as the doors slid open. They were in luck! There were no security guards.

Diesel moved towards the doorway. Peri grabbed his arm to hold him back. 'Wait,' he hissed and pointed to the four cameras aimed at the *Phoenix*. He pulled a small gadget from his pocket. It was round with a red button. 'This will knock out any camera within range. We'll have ten seconds to get on board. Ready?'

Diesel nodded. Peri pressed the button and whispered, 'Now.'

They sprinted to the *Phoenix* and up the ramp.

'Where are Selene and that big ugly dumboid?' Diesel panted as they raced into the ship's mauve-lit corridor.

'I don't know.' Peri wheezed as he spoke. 'They must be hiding somewhere on board. We'll ask the *Phoenix* where.'

As he went to touch a com-pad, it lit up and a message flashed across the screen: *Follow the lights* . . .

At their feet, a series of lights pulsed along the length of the corridor to a portal, lit with a silvery glow.

It opened and, stepping through, they found themselves in a tiny storage room filled with stacks of zero-gravity toilet rolls. 'Selene? Otto?' Diesel shouted. 'It's us!'

Peri heard Selene tut. 'I know! It was *me* who led you here.'

Then the image of the storage cupboard in front of them blinked to reveal a large workshop filled with monitors of every size and shape.

'Come in,' Selene muttered. 'You need to

be on this side of the hologram. I rewired the security systems and this room is no longer on the blueprints.'

There were sleeping bunks at opposite ends of the workshop and bits of electronics equipment scattered everywhere in between. Selene was fiddling with a spiral-shaped device on a workbench. It had a trigger in the middle and a funnel at the other end.

Peri peered at her device. 'What's that you're working on?'

'Don't bother asking her to show you!' Otto shouted. The bumps on his long Meigwor neck bulged with annoyance. 'Inferior device! Doesn't work!'

'It's something my dad and I were trying to perfect,' she said, ignoring the Meigwor bounty hunter.

'Have you been in touch with your dad?' Peri asked, thinking she must be worried about her father. Peri assumed he had been on the IF Space Station when Xion attacked the Milky Way.

Selene huffed. 'If you must know, yes, I have spoken to my dad.' She threw down the wire she was trying to solder. 'Satisfied? Can we drop it?'

Peri was certain she was hiding something, but what? After all they'd been through together, Peri trusted Selene with his life. If she didn't want to talk about her family, he wouldn't push her on it. 'What's the new gadget for?' he asked, changing the subject.

Selene took a deep breath. 'I call it an "electro-pulse". When it's finished, it will be able to fire an electromagnetic wave that disrupts certain types of electronics.'

'Who cares?' Diesel yelled. 'I beat Peri on the final test.'

Otto and Selene shared a look. Then they both burst out laughing.

Diesel put his hands on his hips. 'How dare you? You're mocking the emperor's son. The *victorious* emperor's son, who –'

'Stupid space-monkey!' Otto boomed. 'Selene hacked into the main computers! We saw the whole race! You lost!'

'What do you know, you long-necked

freak?' Diesel shouted. 'I won the race. Peri just crossed the finish line first.'

'Who cares about some silly race?' Otto boomed. 'We should be off on another mission by now! You humans are so slow! Meigwor engineers would already have this ship fixed!'

Beep. Beep. Beep. Peri's com-unit sounded.

Peri answered. It was his father. 'Peri, come up to the Bridge. I want to show you the *Phoenix*'s new upgrades.'

Peri shut off the com-unit and turned to Selene. 'If my dad knows I'm here, do you think they've discovered you too?'

'No way,' Selene said. 'It's your bionic connection that gave you away. Even I can't override that.' She smiled. 'Hurry up! I want to know what they're doing to my ship.'

Peri smiled as he ran off. That was more like the Selene he knew.

Chapter 3

'What have you done?' Peri gasped.

It looked like a cosmic tornado had hit the Bridge. His parents were kneeling in the middle of the wreckage surrounded by laser-cutters and space-wrenches. Bundles of cables were sticking out of holes across the Bridge. The *Phoenix*'s control panel was resting upside down, sprouting wires along its entire length. Zip-dials, switches and monitors were scattered everywhere. Peri's circuits tingled in sympathy with the ship. It was as if part of him had been ripped out and put on display.

His father stood up. He smoothed down his lab-suit as he pulled a couple of capacitors out of his hair.

'We're almost done,' he said. 'We've been carrying out repairs and upgrades.'

Peri stared at the mess. It looked more like they had been trying to destroy everything.

'You'll love the new teleportation feature,' his father continued. 'You can beam yourselves instantly to any part of the ship.'

His mother pointed to a large metallic box. 'We just need to finish installing the Red Helix device and then she's ready to go.'

'What was wrong with the Blue Helix?' Peri asked. On their way back to the solar system, the Blue Helix had saved all their lives by allowing the *Phoenix* to travel back in time by a few seconds. Without it, the ship would have exploded in a vortex.

His mother bent over and started shuffling through a pile of space-o-metric diagrams and circuitry plans. 'I have a chart here somewhere. The Red Helix is even more sophisticated. We discovered a special particle that –'

Peri's father interrupted. 'We shouldn't be telling him. It's top secret.'

'But I have to fly the ship,' Peri objected. 'Surely I should know how it works?'

Peri's father shook his head. 'The Red Helix must only be used as an absolute last resort. You don't need to know what it does. Your bionic connection will sense if you need to use it.'

'So why did you ask me to come up here?' Peri asked.

'Because,' his mother replied, ruffling his hair, 'it's *your* turn for an upgrade.'

Peri's stomach buzzed with fear. 'Upgrade?'

'We know what we're doing, Peri,' his father said. 'We did create your bionic circuits! We just need to check you over. We've learned a lot from your first trip out with the *Phoenix* and we've got some improvements to your bionic abilities.'

'We'll deactivate all your pain protocols,' his mother said. 'You won't feel a thing.'

Looking around the Bridge, Peri couldn't help worrying what having an upgrade might involve, but he trusted his parents. He nodded.

'*Phoenix,*' his father ordered, 'activate Experiment Tune-up Protocol.'

Peri braced himself as the ship's robotic arms swept down from the ceiling and picked him up.

Shhhhuuupt! A black-cushioned table slid out from underneath the 360-monitor and the *Phoenix* rested him on it. Instantly thick straps flew around him and pinned him to the table.

Peri wrestled against the restraints. 'What on Neptune are you doing?'

'Relax,' his mother said, rushing to Peri's side. She stroked his head. 'This is for your own safety, to keep you perfectly still.'

Then his mother pushed a wire up his nose. There was a flash of burning pain. He closed his eyes. Ones and zeros raced through his mind. Computer code! Peri felt dizzy and detached from his body. His parents' voices sounded far away — as if he wasn't really in the room.

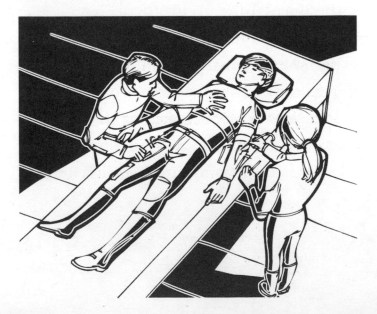

'All upgrade protocols activated,' his father said.

Peri could feel his connection with the *Phoenix* strengthen. His thoughts seemed to leave his body and flood into the ship's computer. His mind stumbled through blueprints and computer logs. Suddenly, he saw a black-and-white image of the Bridge. He was peering at it through the ship's security cameras. He could see his own body lying on the table. His parents were removing components and circuits along his arms, legs and chest. They were replacing them with new, smaller ones.

His parents moved on to his head, using a flesh-healing nano-beam to repair his skin as they went.

'Peri.' His mother looked at the *Phoenix*'s Bridge camera. 'We need you back inside your body for the last bit of the upgrade.'

Peri moved his thoughts back into his body. His limbs were still numb, but he could see again. He blinked, hoping his parents were almost done.

'Good,' his father said. 'You've just tested your tri-quad-quantum connection with the *Phoenix*. Now, tell us about the bionic abilities you've already discovered.'

Peri thought back over his adventures. 'Um . . . the Fight-or-Flight response?'

His mother nodded. 'Good! Fight-or-Flight gives you temporary superhuman strength and speed.'

His father tapped his computer pad. 'We've increased those superhuman abilities by a hundred and ninety-four per cent, and we've improved your capacity to self-generate energy. You're much more efficient now. No more battery problems!'

'You still need to eat properly and get

plenty of sleep,' his mother added. 'You are only *part* bionic. Your human side needs looking after too. It wouldn't hurt to eat some vegetables. I've seen your food-log – too much space-cream.'

'What food-log?' Peri asked.

His mother tutted. 'Your bionic systems record everything you eat.'

Peri scowled. *I've been betrayed by my own bionic body!*

'Give Peri a break,' his father said. 'His circuitry is the most sophisticated technology available. It can handle a little treat –'

The lights on the Bridge flashed as an announcement rang out. *'General Pegg orders Peri and Diesel to the Command Centre within the next ten minutes. Nine minutes and fifty-eight seconds remaining.'*

Peri's father disconnected him and helped

him up from the table. 'We'd better wrap this all up.'

His mother was concentrating on sealing up his skin with the nano-beam.

'There,' his mother said. 'Ready for action!'

Shrrruppt. Diesel appeared on the Bridge. 'Er, hello,' he said hurriedly to Peri's parents, then turned to Peri. 'Come on. We've got to go.' Without waiting for a response, Diesel started to run.

Peri raced after him and out of the *Phoenix*. He caught up with him just as he left the launch bay.

'What do you think General Pegg wants?' Peri asked.

'Probably wants to kick you out of the IFA for being a wastoid.'

'You don't think they know about Selene and Otto?' Peri whispered.

'If they do, it's entirely your fault,' Diesel said. 'I was all for leaving them behind in the Ubi galaxy. They've got to make me a Star Fighter after I whipped you on that obstacle course.'

'I crossed the finish line first,' Peri reminded him.

Diesel just smirked. 'Show me the scores to prove it.'

Peri wished it was that simple. General Pegg didn't seem to really care about their scores. He wasn't happy with either Peri or Diesel.

And that meant trouble.

Chapter 4

Peri and Diesel sprinted to the nearest transport-tube.

'Come on,' Peri yelled, jabbing the command-deck button repeatedly until the doors finally closed. 'General Pegg's temper is not going to get better if we keep him waiting.'

Ping! Before the transport-tube doors had fully opened, Peri and Diesel dashed out. They raced down the almost empty command-deck corridor.

They flashed their passes to the armed

guards outside the Command Centre. As the doors opened, Peri was overwhelmed by the noise. The room was packed with top-ranking IF officers and diplomats shouting to be heard over each other. On a platform towards the front of the room was Diesel's dad, Emperor Elliotte. He was seated in a gilded commander's chair talking to the Venusian ambassador. They were pointing at the holographic map of the solar system that dominated the ceiling.

General Pegg caught their eye and came over. 'Peri, Diesel,' he said. 'Stay where you are and remain silent.'

Peri froze. Everyone had stopped talking and started staring at them. He dreaded to think what the general was going to say next.

'Serjeant-at-arms, step forward,' General Pegg ordered.

An officer in a pristine ceremonial uniform marched towards them. He wore white gloves and held something shiny and silver in his hands. Was it handcuffs? Peri's stomach tightened and he struggled to swallow. Had the IF found out about Selene and Otto?

General Pegg straightened up. 'I've made a decision.'

Peri couldn't breathe. This was it – the moment he would find out whether he was going to achieve his greatest dream.

'Star Fighters are known not only for their bravery and skill, but for their personal honour and respect,' the general began. 'They uphold the laws of the Intergalactic Force and live to the highest moral standards.'

Peri couldn't stand the suspense. What was General Pegg saying?

The serjeant-at-arms handed something to the general. 'Peri, Diesel —' The general paused and studied the pair. 'You have passed all your tests with flying colours. But you only become Star Fighters if you are the bravest and best in the galaxy.'

The general opened his hands to reveal two titanium IF Star Fighter badges. Peri resisted the urge to punch the air.

'Congratulations to the IF's newest and youngest Star Fighters!'

Peri couldn't stop grinning as the general pinned the badge to his uniform. 'It's as much an honour for me to present you these badges as it is for you to wear them. Please pledge your allegiance by reciting the IF creed.'

Peri couldn't believe what was happening. It was the most space-tastic moment of his life. He and Diesel recited the creed

in unison: 'I swear to honour and uphold the laws of the Intergalactic Force. I promise to lay down my life to protect our planets and citizens from greed, corruption and enemies. With every breath in my body, I pledge my loyalty to –'

'– the emperor,' said Peri, just as Diesel boomed, '– my father.'

General Pegg beamed at them. 'You're now members of the most elite peacekeeping force in the universe!'

Instantly the room erupted into loud cheers of 'Peace in space'.

Diesel's hair had turned royal purple with pride.

'We did it!' Peri exclaimed as he high-fived Diesel.

As the cheers died down, the general beckoned them closer. He leaned down, speaking quietly. 'I must admit, I wish you could train for longer. And, to be honest, I'm not completely convinced that you are mature enough to be Star Fighters. But you did a remarkable job in the Ubi galaxy. And, well, we have an urgent mission for you – so what choice is there?'

General Pegg handed what looked like a Martian toadstool to Peri. The flat-dome top was green and covered in red dots. There was a ring of flashing blue lights around the rim. Under the dome, the grey stalk was lined with computer slots. Peri stared at it, wondering what it was.

'It's your Mission Capsule. You plug it into the *Phoenix* and it will brief you on your mission,' the general explained, then he turned and addressed the entire crowd. 'Peri and Diesel's first mission will be to capture a notorious pirate.'

Space pirates! Peri couldn't believe his luck. What an exciting mission! He turned the Mission Capsule over in his hand. Everything he needed to know about his first official Star Fighter mission was inside. He couldn't wait to get started!

'Keep your Mission Capsule plugged in at all times,' said General Pegg. 'It will observe your progress and report back to me. No more time to celebrate, I'm afraid. Go — you have a difficult task ahead. Time is of the essence!'

Peri turned to collect Diesel, but he had vanished! Maybe he had already returned to the *Phoenix*, eager to get going on their first mission.

Peri raced out of the Command Centre, trying not to grin too foolishly as he thought, *I'm a real Star Fighter now!*

Chapter 5

Sirens blared as Peri raced down the base-ship's corridors, heading back towards the *Phoenix*. Now he had their Mission Capsule there was no time to waste!

He tore around a corner and spotted Diesel arguing with his father, the emperor. Peri skidded to a halt and darted behind the open access panel to one of the service tunnels. Luckily they were too busy argu-ing to notice him.

Peri peered around the edge of the panel. Diesel was shaking his head. The emperor loomed over him, his grey-streaked band of purple hair bristling.

'Take it,' the emperor shouted. 'You're still my son.'

Diesel reached out for something in the emperor's hand. As soon as Peri saw it, he knew what it was – another Mission Capsule! Diesel stuffed it into his pocket. He was clearly unhappy about it.

Why is the emperor giving Diesel a Mission Capsule? Peri wondered.

Before they could discover him, Peri slipped down the service tunnel and out into the launch bay. He ran up the ramp into the *Phoenix*. As he raced down towards the Bridge, the ship's mechanical arms stretched from the walls and lifted him into shrink-to-fit Expedition Wear, then reattached his titanium Star Fighter badge before letting him go.

Peri stepped on to the Bridge. His parents had left it spotless. There wasn't a loose wire or circuit board in sight.

Soon Selene and Otto joined them on the Bridge.

'Nice badges, guys!' Selene said, grinning at Peri and Diesel as she took her place. 'We saw it all on the com-screen!'

'Thanks,' said Peri, unable to keep the

smile off his own face. Even the Meigwor bounty hunter was almost smiling, although he was clearly trying not to show it.

'I knew I'd pass,' said Diesel, his chin tilting upwards.

'Congratulations,' said Selene, as her astro-harness clicked into place. 'But I'm *still* in charge of engineering.'

Peri sat down in the captain's chair. 'Everyone ready?' he asked the crew.

'Let's get to work,' said Diesel. Then he noticed that Peri was staring at him. 'What?'

'What was that between you and the emperor?' Peri asked. 'It looked serious.'

Diesel's eyes flashed yellow. 'What I talk about with my father is none of your *dung y'r'ah* business, you bugonaut!' he shouted. 'Star Fighter or not, I'm the emperor's son and I can do whatever the *prrrip'chiq* I like.'

'You can yell as much as you want,' Peri said. 'But, we're a team and we need to start acting as one. If you've forgotten, General Pegg is keeping a close eye on us. Secrets will just get in our way.'

'Whatever,' muttered Diesel. 'Let's just *go*.'

Peri clicked his fingers and the control panel hovered closer. A compartment slid open to reveal a round socket for the Mission Capsule. Peri placed the mushroom-shaped device in the hole. Tiny metal claws sprang out and twisted it into place. The circle of blue lights around the rim turned red. A green light flickered above the capsule and a hologram of General Pegg appeared.

'This mission is for IF eyes only,' he said. 'Star Fighters Peri and Diesel, your mission is to capture the space pirate Jaxx, who escaped during the Xion attack before he

could stand trial for an intergalactic crime spree that resulted in the theft of the Heart of Mars.'

Selene coughed.

'In addition we believe he has stolen over three hundred space vessels and kidnapped dozens of local officials. He is the most ruthless, cold-hearted criminal in the universe. The IF has declared him Space Enemy Number One!'

Selene shifted in her seat and coughed again.

Peri paused the hologram. 'You OK, Selene?'

'I'm fine,' she muttered.

Peri let the mission briefing continue. 'All relevant data has been uploaded to the *Phoenix*,' said the general. 'You will first travel to the last known coordinates of the IF ship Jaxx stole during his escape. Good luck!'

As the hologram vanished, the coordinates appeared on the monitor. It was a location way outside the solar system.

'Space pirates are the lowest of the low!' Diesel sneered. 'They should all be fed to Venusian bog beasts.'

'You don't even know if Jaxx really is a space pirate,' said Selene. 'He's innocent until *proven* guilty. We shouldn't jump to conclusions.'

'You have to admit,' Peri said, 'running away before his trial does make Jaxx look awfully guilty.'

'Perhaps he's trying to find evidence to show he is innocent,' Selene replied.

Peri shook his head. 'He's going the wrong way about it if he is. Besides, it's not our mission to decide whether he's innocent. Our orders are to find and arrest him.' Peri flexed his fingers as he looked over the control panel. He could feel his connection with the ship strengthening. 'Prepare for take-off.'

His hands darted across the panel, flicking switches and twisting zip-dials. It was good to be back in command of the *Phoenix*. He let his palm rest on the pyramid-shaped button and then pushed it down. Peri felt the vibrations from the engines rise up through the vessel and into his body. He felt at one with the ship. 'Let's go catch a space pirate!'

As the massive launch-bay doors slid open, the *Phoenix* roared into space.

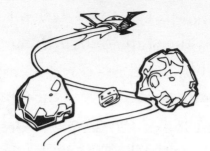

Chapter 6

Peri stared at the 360-monitor as a rock two hundred times bigger than the *Phoenix* tumbled past. *Crraaaa-aarroorrr!* It smashed into another asteroid and obliterated it, leaving behind nothing but space dust.

Peri swallowed. They'd just flown across seven galaxies, had near misses with three black holes, and for what? To risk their lives in the largest asteroid field he'd ever seen.

'Welcome to the Rumana galaxy, guys,' Peri muttered.

'This has to be a mistake,' Diesel said.

'Why would General Pegg send us here? Check those coordinates again.'

'The IF must have got their intelligence wrong,' Selene said.

It didn't look promising, but orders were orders. Peri's hands darted over the control panel. 'Activating a full scan.'

'It's no use,' Selene said. 'Jaxx is obviously not here.'

'We should lie in wait!' Otto boomed.

Diesel scoffed. 'That's just a fancy way of saying we should hide.'

Otto's long neck bulged with anger. 'Meigwors don't hide! We lie in wait! We set traps!'

Ping! A light on the console flashed to show the scan was complete. Peri brought up the results on screen. He could see nothing but rocks, and no sign of any spacecraft.

But Jaxx had to be here somewhere. The IF

had tracked the space pirate's stolen spaceship to these coordinates. There must be a clue to his whereabouts. 'Perhaps Jaxx has a secret base hidden close by?' Peri suggested.

'We'd never find it among the asteroids,' Selene replied. 'If he is here, he's chosen the most brilliant of hiding places.'

'That's it!' said Peri, his circuits tingling excitedly. 'Jaxx is on the run – which means he wants to avoid detection. I bet he's using cloaking technology to hide his spacecraft from IF scanners.'

Peri's hands darted over the control panel. He knew how to find Jaxx! Even a cloaked ship left a gravitational wake. He slammed the button to refocus the *Phoenix*'s detectors. He only had to wait a nanosecond before – *ping!* – a fast-moving object appeared on the screen.

'I've found something!' Peri called. He

zoomed in on the foreign object as it zigzagged between the asteroids, weaving from one icy rock to the other. It was a hunter class stealth ship.

'Definitely pirates!' Otto shouted. 'They prefer small vessels! Blast it!'

Peri turned to Otto. 'We're here to capture Jaxx, not kill him,' he said. He turned back to the scanners. 'Hey . . . where did he go?'

'You lost the target?' Diesel exclaimed. 'What a lamizoid!'

Peri checked the scanners again, but there was no trace of the craft. 'No . . . it just . . . vanished.'

Ping! Another stealth ship appeared and then disappeared.

Peri frowned. 'Something very strange is going on here.' He began tracing the heat signatures of the ships. There had to be a clue as to what was happening to those ships. Slowly, dotted lines appeared on the 360-monitor to show where the ships had been. Both lines led to a huge asteroid in the centre of the field.

Peri pointed. 'That's what they were heading towards.'

'It must be Haven!' Otto boomed. 'The legendary hollow asteroid.'

'That's just a myth,' Selene said.

'No!' Otto shouted. 'Haven is a free port for smugglers and pirates! It's run by the Mezzoka Clan!'

Diesel scoffed. 'Are you saying that an organised clan of the worst criminals in the Milky Way runs a secret base out of a hollow asteroid?'

'There's only one way to find out,' Peri said.

He reconfigured the *Phoenix*'s scanners to penetrate deep into the asteroid. But all that showed up on screen was the word *Error* in angry red letters. 'There's definitely some-thing ultra-high-tech there,' he said. 'Only the most advanced force field would be strong enough to block the *Phoenix*'s scanners.'

'We should leave,' Selene said. 'If Otto's right, we're heading for big trouble.'

Otto shook his massive head. 'Let's blast our way in!'

'Blasting isn't always the answer,' Peri said. 'I think we should trick our way inside. We need to disguise the ship, and then go undercover as space criminals.'

A control pad slid out from the main console as if the ship had read his mind. A hologram of the *Phoenix* appeared above it. Peri twisted a zip-dial and the image of the craft shrank a bit and turned pink. He twisted another and its smooth shape became rounder and less sleek.

'I don't think many pirates fly pink ships,'

Selene said. Peri twisted the dial again and punched a few buttons. It wasn't long before the *Phoenix* looked like it had come off worse in several space-battles. Its hull was now black and red, with countless dents and scratches – the perfect disguise for pirates.

'Now for us,' Peri said. 'We can't go around in Expedition Wear.'

'I'll sort it out,' Diesel said, pushing Otto aside and pressing buttons on the control panel. 'We need camouflage and lots of black so we can hide in the shadows and stuff.'

'No!' Otto boomed, elbowing Diesel out of the way. 'I want clothes in the latest Meigwor style! We need greens and blues with ammo-belts and massive weapons!'

'The Meigwors have style?' Diesel scoffed.

'We need to look like successful space pirates,' Peri said.

'Commands accepted,' the *Phoenix* announced calmly. 'Please wait.'

There was a short pause before the ship's robotic arms shot out of the ceiling and grabbed all four crew members. Their Expedition Wear was quickly swapped for dark blue Astro-jeans and tight-fitting black jackets.

'We're ready to go!' Peri slammed the pyramid-shaped button and they blasted off towards Haven. He kept the scanners sweeping the asteroid, looking for a way to get inside, but there was nothing.

Dwoooooooooooo . . .

'What was that noise?' Otto asked.

'I think the engines have stalled,' said Peri, desperately jabbing at the controls.

Eeeee-rrraaaaa. Eeeee-rrraaaa! Sirens sounded across the Bridge. Robotic arms shot from the walls and then sprang back again.

Lights flashed on and off. The control panel swung away from Peri and rose up into the air. Artificial gravity turned off and on again, throwing them into the air before dropping them back on the deck.

'We're being scanned,' Selene shouted as a yellow light flashed through the Bridge. 'Everything has gone haywire! I can't stop it.'

'Fight it, *Phoenix*,' Peri urged.

But before he could do anything else, a blinding light exploded through the Bridge.

Chapter 7

The ship was in total darkness. Peri clicked his fingers, but the control panel didn't respond. He couldn't feel his bionic connection with the ship. His hands turned cold with fear as he realised the ship was completely without power.

What had happened to the *Phoenix*?

'We're under attack!' Otto shouted. 'We must fight!'

'Stay calm,' Peri yelled. 'We need to restore power.'

'Working on it,' came Selene's muffled yelp somewhere in the dark.

Two beams of light sliced across the Bridge. Otto and Diesel were in the cosmic-combat position, torches in one hand and zapsters in the other. One of the beams caught Selene's legs wiggling into a hole in the deck.

'An alien intruder has captured Selene!' Otto boomed. 'I blast!'

'Wait!' Peri yelled. 'Selene is below deck trying to restore power.'

Otto lowered his blaster. 'Are you sure?'

'Yes!' There was a flicker of light across the Bridge. Peri ran to the control panel and started activating every sensor he could think of. 'We don't have full systems. The sensors are dead. Diesel, check weapons.'

Diesel was already flicking switches at

the gunnery station. '*S'fâh*,' he yelled as he thumped it. 'We're defenceless!'

Selene pulled herself back on to the Bridge. 'It's a dampening field round the ship,' she explained. 'We've not sustained any actual damage. Whoever attacked us doesn't want to destroy us. They're restoring systems one by one.'

As she spoke, the 360-monitor sprang to life. They could see that they were actually inside the asteroid! The *Phoenix* was surrounded by a flickering blue electro-fence. Everywhere Peri looked he could see space vessels of different shapes and sizes jostling for room behind the electrified barrier. Beyond the fence, jutting from the far side of the asteroid, was a settlement of squat, ramshackle buildings and the odd space rocket.

A green-skinned horned Venusian in a

blue sash appeared on the screen and hissed at them like a Martian lizard. Peri pressed the slight bulge under his chin and activated his SpeakEasy computer chip. The translation device crackled loudly before Peri found the right wavelength. 'Language frequency 23.10.04,' Peri told the others.

Diesel adjusted his SpeakEasy implant as Selene and Otto strapped two battered

SpeakEasy devices to their heads. Now they could all hear what the Venusian was saying: 'Haven Security. All ships visiting Haven must be inspected by security teams. Please grant permission to board your vessel or exercise your right to be destroyed.'

Peri hit the mute button. 'Otto is our best chance of getting in. They won't suspect him of being an IF agent.'

Diesel nodded. Otto had been a bounty hunter on planet Meigwor. 'He'll probably blend right in on Haven.'

'Yes!' Otto boomed. 'Follow my lead, space-monkeys! I know how to deal with the criminal world!'

Peri reactivated the communications channel.

Otto took a deep breath. 'Listen –'

'Stand by,' the Haven security guard replied. 'Beaming aboard.'

With a blaze of fizzy orange light, the security officer appeared. He had a blaster in each hand. He looked around the Bridge.

'Haven welcomes you,' he said as he holstered his weapons.

Otto licked his lipless mouth. 'Keep your welcome! Just lead me to the trouble!'

The security guard straightened his sash. 'No weapons, or personal defence devices, are allowed on Haven. You must obey the rules. Haven was established to allow the exchange of goods and services away from prying eyes, not as a place for trouble-making. Honour among thieves is strictly enforced here. Understood?'

Otto nodded and the guard carried on: 'The atmosphere has been configured to be safe for all species. And we value privacy. We don't want to know your names. No one will give you theirs or tell you where they're from. So don't even ask. Everyone enters Haven at his, her, or its, own risk. There are no peacekeepers, no police and no IF here. Do you agree to these terms?'

'Of course!' Otto boomed. 'My crew and I are no strangers to places like these.'

'Stand together for beaming.' The security guard turned to Selene. 'You must leave that device behind. It's been identified as a weapon.'

Selene looked at her electro-pulse gadget, which she was holding in her hands. 'But —'

Peri put a hand on Selene's shoulder. 'Don't argue,' he hissed. 'It doesn't work yet anyway.'

Selene put her gadget down and stood with the rest of the crew. The guard pulled what looked like a remote control from his pocket and fired it at them.

An orange teleportation beam fizzed

around the crew. It tingled against Peri's skin and the orange light covered his eyes. He felt like an astro-mint in a bottle of Saturn Soda. Then, nanoseconds later, the beam vanished and Peri found himself on a metal teleportation platform in the middle of Haven. He looked out across

the vast interior of the asteroid. On the other side, he could see the *Phoenix* waiting for them behind the blue electro-fence.

'Get a move on!' said a guard in a green sash. 'Other people need to use the teleportation platform!'

As Peri and his crew hurried away from the platform, a thin man with more scars than money ran beside Otto. 'Need a better crew, captain? They look on the small side.'

'No, no!' Otto pushed him away. 'They're useless, but they're my crew and I'm keeping them!'

'Useless?' Diesel snarled. 'How dare you –'

'Keep quiet, space-monkey!' said Otto as he led them into the heart of Haven.

It was hard weaving through the streets. Everyone was elbowing and shoving their way forward. Peri peeked through an open door in one of the shacks that lined the streets. Two tough-looking aliens sat inside, deep in conversation. One of them opened a wide astro-case. Peri caught a glint of gold, before the alien noticed him and slammed the case shut. His glare was enough to make Peri slip away quickly and not look back.

Every street corner had buskers or pirates arguing — sometimes both. The whole place stank of stale drink, sweat and open drains.

Peri pulled his crew aside. 'I picked up some short-range coms-patches from the *Phoenix*,' he whispered. He pulled the postage-stamp-sized devices from his pocket. They had delicate gold circuitry on one side and chameleo-skin on the other.

He handed them out. 'Stick one behind your ear. It'll blend into your skin, and they'll allow us to communicate with each other. Without our Expedition Wear, we'll need them if we get separated.'

Peri stuck his coms-patch on. He heard a loud whistling in his ear as the device connected to his circuits and his brain. The whistling vanished and a menu of options appeared in his mind's eye: *Open Radio, Close Radio, Track Others, Transmit Image.*

Peri mentally chose the last option. He'd uploaded an image of Jaxx into his coms-patch before leaving the ship. 'I'm sending you all a photo of Jaxx.'

The space pirate flashed across Peri's vision like a ghost. He was looking at Selene, but he could see Jaxx's face hovering over her. The space pirate looked really familiar as if he'd met him somewhere before.

'Will you stop looking at me?' Selene huffed.

Peri shook his head and the image of Jaxx faded. 'Haven's huge. We should start searching.'

'This way,' Otto shouted, pointing towards the roughest-looking area of the market-place. The streets were even narrower, as if the shacks had been pushed together by a trash compactor. The buildings seemed to have been made from whatever their alien owners could find – shipping crates, bits of spacecraft, sheet metal and tarpaulins. Smoke and the sound of arguing drifted through the gaps in their walls.

'How are we going to find him in there?' Diesel asked.

'I have found more elusive prey in harder places,' Otto boomed. 'This is child's play.'

As they followed Otto down the alley-way, Diesel muttered, 'Meigwors have strange childhoods.'

Peri tried not to laugh. 'Everything about Meigwors is strange,' he said. But he was worried about how they were going to find Jaxx. They couldn't disappoint General Pegg. They had to locate Jaxx and this was their only lead. Peri wasn't about to let his first official Star Fighter mission end in failure.

Chapter 8

'Mind your own business or I'll blast you into space,' snarled an alien with a dozen eyes.

Peri swallowed as he backed off into the crowd, hoping the alien wouldn't come after him. It was really hard to search for anyone on Haven. No one on this asteroid liked to make eye contact unless they absolutely had to.

At the next crossroads, Peri stopped his crew. 'We're attracting too much attention as a group. Let's split up. Selene, head back to the teleportation platform and keep watch. Otto, go left. Diesel, go right. I'll carry on in this direction. Use your coms-patches to keep in touch.'

Peri set off, but the alleys got narrower and darker as they twisted down and down into the worst part of Haven. The smell of sewage became almost unbearable. But before he decided to turn back, Peri spot-ted a crowded tavern.

The perfect place to find a space pirate!

Peri sneaked along the outside of the tavern, peeking through the gaps in the tarpaulin sides. Tired-looking waitresses carried large trays filled with glasses that brimmed with a foul-smelling liquid and dishes piled high with fried space-rats on sticks. There was no sign of Jaxx. Two humans with scars over their faces and burns on their arms were talking close to the tarpaulin. They had to be space pirates. Peri edged closer to eavesdrop. He listened for a while. He could only hear snatches of their conversation.

'. . . IF ship for sale . . .' The words triggered an internal alarm. Peri leaned in.

'I've never seen a real IF ship,' one pirate said. 'But I bet it's a perfect replacement for our rust bucket.'

The other pirate was halfway through crunching into a fried rat. 'Can't be a real one, can it?' The pirate spat tiny flecks of fried rat as he spoke. 'We'll check it out, but I want to eat first.'

'Yeah, all right. The guy selling it hangs around outside the Probe Palace. He should be there for a while.'

Peri couldn't believe his luck. He activated the coms-patch. 'Someone's trying to sell an IF ship. It has to be Jaxx,' he whispered. 'Otto, the seller does business around the Probe Palace. See if you can find out where it is. I'll round up the others. We'll meet you there.'

'Maybe later,' Diesel replied. 'I'm in the middle of buying something.'

'That sounds like a long shot, Peri,' Selene chipped in. 'And I'm in a good place to watch people coming and going. Jaxx is bound to pass me if he's here.'

Peri sighed. *Why aren't they listening to me?* He would have to go and collect them. He activated the location-trackers on the coms-patch. An arrow appeared in his field of vision and Peri started jogging in that direction. He weaved through the streets until he found Diesel in the middle of a small crowd, haggling with an old man.

'Come on,' Peri said, pulling Diesel away. 'We've got to go.'

'*Pŏr'süng*, Peri,' Diesel hissed. 'I've got him down to ten squares. You have to be pretty clever not to fall for their tricks. They always start too high.' Diesel turned, but the old man and the crowd had melted away. Diesel patted down his pockets, then gasped. '*S'fâh*, all my squares are gone. I've been robbed!'

Peri dragged the half-Martian away before he could cause more trouble.

They found Selene crouched by the teleporters, watching people arrive and depart. She shrugged and followed them.

Peri activated his coms-patch. 'Otto, any luck finding the Probe Palace?'

'Yes!' Otto boomed over the coms-patch. 'It's a large casino next to a used-spaceship yard! Transmitting coordinates now.'

A map flashed across Peri's mind's eye. 'Come on,' he said.

Peri led Selene and Diesel back through the streets of Haven until they came to a tall, tapered building that towered over the others. A sign saying *Probe Palace Casino* hung over the door. Otto was waiting for them outside. He pointed to a squat orange alien with a mouth full of gold teeth who was standing at the entrance to the used-spaceship yard.

'That's Awdus Erox, the spaceship dealer!'

Otto boomed. 'I bet he bought the ship from Jaxx hoping to sell it for a lot more!'

'But why would Jaxx abandon a decent ship?' Diesel said.

'He must suspect the IF is tracking him,' Peri said. 'But he's always a step ahead of us. Someone must be helping –'

'What do we do now?' Selene interrupted.

'The ship is our only lead,' Peri said. 'Diesel, Otto, you guys pretend you're interested in buying it. That will create a diversion, then Selene and I can sneak on board to snoop around.'

As Diesel and Otto started haggling with Awdus, Peri and Selene tiptoed past. The IF ship was made of sleek grey and yellow panels. It wasn't big, but it looked fast and well designed. It was definitely the best ship in the yard.

'This way,' Selene said as she shinned up

one of the ship's metal landing struts.

She pulled out an electro-wrench from her pocket and removed an access panel, then helped Peri up into the ship and on to the Bridge. Inside, it was a mess. The deck was covered in wires, components and strange-looking gadgets.

'I think Jaxx was taking apart the consoles,' Selene muttered, almost to herself.

'See if you can figure out what he was trying to do,' Peri said. 'I'll check the computers.'

He activated the main console. The flight data confirmed that the ship had escaped just before the IF Space Station had exploded. Peri searched for more, but there was little else in the memory. Jaxx had done a good job erasing the data, especially the security feed. Peri hunted around the ship's programming for anything that the space pirate might have overlooked.

'Gotcha!' Peri found a back-up flight plan on the system. His neck tingled as he pulled it up on screen. Jaxx was planning to intercept a comet close to the rings of Saturn.

But that didn't make sense. Why was Jaxx returning to the solar system and not running as far away as he could?

Peri turned to ask Selene what she thought, but she was fiddling with some sort of gadget. It looked a bit like her electro-pulse device, but she'd been made to leave that behind on the *Phoenix*.

'What have you found?' he asked.

Selene quickly shoved the device into a bag. 'Nothing useful.'

Peri frowned. *Why is she acting so weirdly?* he wondered.

'Did you find anything?' she asked.

Peri nodded. 'A flight plan. I think Jaxx is heading for the rings of Saturn.'

'We'd better get going then,' Selene replied, slinging the bag over her shoulder and heading for the exit hatch.

Peri ran after her and they raced back to collect the others.

Diesel and Otto were still arguing with Awdus Erox.

'Let's go,' Peri said.

'Not now, Peri!' Diesel shouted. 'This ship is almost ours. We're down to a thousand squares.'

'It's not worth more than nine hundred squares!' Otto boomed.

'Nine hundred squares?!' Awdus Erox spluttered. 'That's daylight astrobbery!'

'Don't you know how to haggle?' Diesel asked him. 'You couldn't sell space to an astronaut.'

'Is that so?' Awdus Erox huffed. 'I sold a sleek one-person craft earlier today. It was a sweet deal, part-exchanged for that ship.'

Awdus must have sold it to Jaxx, thought Peri. A one-person craft would be perfect for intercepting a comet. 'We've got to go — now!' he told his friends.

'You and your precious Star Fighter mission!' Otto boomed, shaking his head.

Awdus Erox gulped. 'You're Star Fighters!?'

Before any of them could react, Awdus had run off and there was a yell from a large pirate close by. 'Star Fighters . . . Get them!'

Peri spun around. There were three pirates armed with metal poles charging at them. 'Smash the Star Fighters!' one of them hollered.

'Run!' Peri screamed.

Shouts for Star Fighters' blood followed them as they fled. Otto took the lead,

shoving aside anyone who got in his way. Peri leaped and dodged the aliens who had fallen as he ran, making sure Diesel and Selene were keeping up with them.

The mob was getting louder as they knocked over stalls and crashed into people. Diesel, now ahead of Peri, stumbled. Something clattered to the ground from Diesel's pocket and Peri snatched it up. He jumped over a sewer ditch and kept running. Peri glanced down at the object in his hands. It looked like the Mission Capsule Diesel's father had given him. But there was no time to think about it. Peri raced on, hoping he'd survive the angry crowd long enough to find out the secret Diesel was keeping.

Chapter 9

'Hurry!' Peri yelled to Selene. 'The mob's catching up!'

Diesel was already on a teleportation platform. He was fighting back angry aliens who were trying to stop Otto taking over the controls. Peri stuffed the Mission Capsule into his jacket pocket so Diesel wouldn't see it. Then he shoved through the queue of aliens and ran on to the platform with Selene right behind him. As he and Selene skidded to a halt, Peri shouted, 'Let's get out of here!'

Otto slammed on the controls and they were beamed aboard the *Phoenix*.

Peri jumped into the captain's chair and hit the pyramid-shaped button to fire up the engines. 'Selene,' he said, 'override Haven's security and beam us out of here!'

'Already on it,' she yelled as her hands darted over the controls. A flash of bright light filled the Bridge and then vanished. They were back in outer space.

With a twist of a zip-dial Peri removed the *Phoenix*'s disguise, then pulled down the thrusters and set their speed to maximum. As soon as they were clear of Haven, he planned to find out what was on Diesel's Mission Capsule.

'Something's following us,' Diesel said. 'They're too small and fast to be ships or drones. Magnifying now!'

A black-and-yellow mist appeared on the

screen. As the 360-monitor zoomed in, Peri saw thousands of small robotic wasps swarming towards them.

'Zespa!' Selene cried. 'My dad told me about them. Their wings are made from ultra-sharp blades and will tear through the *Phoenix* like a photon beam through ice. Activate shields.'

'*Ch'açh!*' Diesel exclaimed as the cloud of Zespa grew larger and wider. 'Haven's scanners have damaged our shields too! They won't take many hits.'

'We're going to have to outrun the Zespa!' Peri grabbed the Nav-wheel and fired the thrusters. It was going to take all his ability to outrun a million robot wasps in an enormous asteroid field.

Something sleek and metallic caught his eye. It was a small, one-man fighter, blasting away from Haven.

'Jaxx!' Peri yelled and pointed at the 360-monitor. 'Otto and Diesel, start shooting Zespa!' Peri swung the *Phoenix* round to follow Jaxx. Within seconds, Otto was blasting with the *Phoenix*'s quantum-blaster.

Chung-Tung-Tung! Shoow-waaawk!

Diesel was firing the laser cannon. 'Seventy destroyed!' he yelled.

'That's nothing!' Otto shouted. 'Two hundred vaporised.'

Chung-Tung-Tung! Shoow-waaawk!

'Three hundred obliterated!' Diesel yelled.

Peri swerved around a space-rock, then dodged more Zespa. They were everywhere. Every time he spun around an asteroid more deadly creatures were waiting. It wouldn't take long before they'd overwhelm the ship and Jaxx's craft was getting further and further away.

'I've got something that might help,' Selene said. 'An electro-pulse!'

'But it's never worked properly,' Peri hissed. 'This is not the time to test out a new gizmo!'

'Trust me!' Instead of reaching for the gadget she had left on board when they teleported on to Haven, Selene pulled a different one from her bag. It was almost identical. It was the device he had seen Selene fiddling with on Jaxx's ship and then hidden from him.

Peri wove in and out through the swarm of Zespa, narrowly missing an asteroid. They didn't have much choice – it was Selene's device or nothing. He nodded at her. 'Give it a try!'

Selene activated the electro-pulse.

Huummm-mmm-MMM! Beep-Beep-BEEEEP!

Its strange racket got louder and louder,

and then went completely silent before a blinding flash of blue light erupted from the gadget. Peri's eyes flickered and his body twitched as the pulse crackled through him and out into space.

In an instant, the Zespa were nothing more than floating dots spiralling slowly away through space.

'*Mars'rakk!*' Diesel cheered as he high-fived Otto. 'Selene, I can't believe it worked. How did a wastoid like you manage that?'

'It was nothing. Just some . . .' Selene looked away. 'Hey, where's Jaxx?'

Peri activated the long-range scanners. They showed . . . nothing.

'He's escaped!' Otto boomed.

'Not for long,' Peri said. 'I know where he's heading. If we use Superluminal speed, we can beat him to the rings of Saturn.'

Peri slid open the red Superluminal panel

and punched in the coordinates. He flicked the switch and the *Phoenix* moved faster than light itself. As the view in the 360-monitor blurred into a swirling pattern of starlight, Peri felt for the Mission Capsule in his pocket. He looked around. Diesel and Otto were comparing footage of their Zespa-blasting. Selene was fiddling with her gadget again. They were distracted, but Peri knew they'd notice if he slipped away. He didn't have much time before they reached Saturn. And he needed to see what Diesel's Mission Capsule said before they got there. He didn't want any more surprises.

His hands tingled as a button labelled *Sneak-o-Cloak* flashed on the controls. He smacked it and saw a faint shimmering green field of energy projected from the control panel. As the light stretched past,

Peri's bionic connection told him it would hide his actions from the rest of the crew. As long as no one walked right up to him, all the others would see was a hologram of Peri just sitting in the chair.

A monitor whirled up from the arm of his chair and a Mission Capsule reader popped out of the top of it. Peri plugged Diesel's capsule into place. Peri channelled the sound into his coms-patch. The screen flickered, before the stern-faced emperor appeared.

'My son . . . you must get the Heart of Mars back at any cost!' The emperor pointed to a jewel as big as one of Otto's fists. It glowed with an orange radiance. It was stunning. Distracted, Peri didn't notice Diesel walk over and step suddenly through the Sneak-o-Cloak.

'Will you tell Otto –' Diesel stopped and his eyes flashed yellow. 'That's *my* Mission Capsule!'

Diesel lunged, but Peri grabbed the capsule first and slipped out of the chair. 'You should have shared this with me. We're Star Fighters, and we're friends.'

'Give it back. You've no right to look at it,' Diesel shouted, kicking the chair. 'My father swore me to secrecy. He blames the Xion attack for the Heart of Mars being stolen, and thinks that all Martians will be cursed until it's returned. I have to find it and you can't stop me.'

Peri sighed and handed the Mission Capsule back. 'Diesel, didn't you think I would want to help you?'

'Stealing my Mission Capsule was a strange way to go about it!' Diesel growled. 'I don't need any help, but ... having a lamizoid like you on my side wouldn't hurt, I guess.'

Peri glanced up at the 360-monitor. Saturn, the dusty gas giant, was beginning to fill the entire screen. Sunlight glinted off its wide, revolving ice rings. 'We won't tell the others,' he said, deactivating the Sneak-o-Cloak.

The green shimmer around them vanished.

'Selene,' Peri said, 'use the Exo-Scanner to look for Jaxx's ship's heat signature.'

'Already on it,' Selene reported. 'Displaying on screen.'

Peri studied the scanner's results. The rings of Saturn were shown as a patchwork of different colours and shades, revealing the coldest and hottest spots. They were all blues and browns, apart from a tiny amber speck. Peri was puzzled that Selene didn't spot it, but there was no time to think.

'There's Jaxx!' Peri pointed and snapped his fingers. The control panel slid under his hands and he fired the sub-light engines. 'If we're quick enough, we can catch him by surprise.'

But as they got closer to the one-man ship, it bolted.

'He's going in at the wrong angle,' Peri shouted and pulled hard on the Nav-wheel, adjusting the *Phoenix*'s position. He watched as Jaxx's ship bounced helplessly between the ice rings. Peri carefully activated the thrusters. As the *Phoenix* surged forward, Jaxx's small craft dived through the rings.

'Diesel, Otto,' Peri shouted, 'we're going through the rings! I need your help to blast a path for us.'

Peri swerved down. The gunners started blasting chunks of ice out of the way. As they came out of the other side of the rings, Jaxx's craft was flying wildly out of control and on a collision course with the planet.

'Something's wrong!' Selene cried.

'Scanners show that Jaxx is injured and unconscious,' Peri reported.

'If I don't do something, he's going to crash!' Selene screamed.

Before Peri could ask the engineer what she meant, Selene had vanished.

Jaxx's ship was lurching between the churning masses of ice. It wasn't going to survive long!

'*Phoenix*,' Peri called, 'find Selene!'

Selene appeared on the monitor inside Jaxx's cramped vessel. She was leaning over the unconscious body of Jaxx, trying to steer his ship. 'I'm doing the best I can, but the ship's too badly damaged,' she yelled. 'You've got to beam us back, Peri!'

Peri's fingers raced across the control panel. He pulled a lever to activate the teleportation beam, but nothing happened.

'It won't work!' Peri cried. 'The mineral deposits in the ice are causing too much interference.'

Selene looked terrified. 'If you don't do something,' she said, 'we're going to die!'

Chapter 10

'Engine's in a critical condition,' Selene yelled. 'Navigation's dead!'

Jaxx's ship spun off the edge of an ice-rock, scattering pieces of the starboard engine across the rings. Peri needed to somehow get the small vessel away from the ice rings' interference. It was the only chance he had of beaming them on to the *Phoenix* before Jaxx's ship crashed or exploded.

This isn't just some stupid obstacle course, Peri thought. *Selene and Jaxx's lives are in my hands!*

'The IF obstacle course!' Peri exclaimed. His mind tingled as he realised he knew what to do. His hands darted across the control panel. He yanked on the thrusters, sending the *Phoenix* hurtling towards the tiny craft.

'Have you lost your bionic mind?' Diesel shouted. 'You're going to get us all killed!'

'Peri!' Selene pleaded. 'Don't do anything stupid!'

'Don't worry,' Peri yelled. 'I've done this before!'

It wasn't going to be easy to intercept Jaxx's out-of-control ship, especially at this speed. He thought he might just be able to snatch them up with a laser net — *if* he could dodge the ice debris . . .

He swerved the ship left, then right. It was just a matter of timing — and hoping that the g-forces involved wouldn't rip both ships apart. He activated the laser net as

the *Phoenix* hurtled towards Jaxx's vessel. Using his bionic connection to make microscopic adjustments, he angled the net to grab the damaged ship.

'Hold on tight!' he yelled to Selene.

The *Phoenix* heaved violently as the laser net snatched up Jaxx's ship. Peri strained against his astro-harness as both vessels were thrown spinning off into space towards Jupiter. But they still weren't far enough from the rings' interference.

'Ten, nine, eight –' Peri counted.

'Peri!' Selene screamed. 'Jaxx is awake, but we're losing engine stability!'

Peri smashed on the emergency thrusters. The *Phoenix* roared forward. The whole Bridge shook from the strain. The laser net was ripped apart by the awesome forces bearing down on it, catapulting Jaxx's ship away from the rings.

'Activating teleporter!' Peri yelled as he slammed down the lever.

A nanosecond later, Jaxx's ship exploded in a fireball the size of a comet.

'S'fâh!' Diesel exclaimed.

Otto bowed his head. 'It was a noble death.'

Peri pulled another lever. Selene and Jaxx rematerialised on the Bridge in a bright shimmer of orange light. They had their arms around each other as if they were wrestling.

'No!' Peri and Diesel leaped from their chairs and grabbed the fugitive. 'Get your hands off her!'

'Death to the pirate!' Otto rushed forward with his silver electro-prod out.

'Wait!' Selene jumped and grabbed Otto's arm. 'It's not what you think.'

'Let go!' Otto yelled, trying to shake

Selene off. The electro-prod swished wildly, sending sparks flying everywhere. As Otto dragged her towards Jaxx, Selene pulled a small tube from her belt and pressed it into the Meigwor's arm.

Otto screamed and dropped his weapon to cradle his arm. 'What was that for? He was trying to hurt you!'

Selene snatched up the electro-prod and pointed it at Otto.

'He was hugging me!' Selene panted. 'Jaxx is my dad!'

'Hugging?' Otto boomed, the splotches around his eyes darkening. 'Awful ... Terrible ... Disgusting human behaviour!'

'Your dad?' Peri let go of Jaxx and stared at him. He could see the family resemblance now. Selene had his eyes and chin. They even had matching smears of grease on their cheeks.

'Is that why he was always ahead of us?' Peri asked.

Selene looked embarrassed. 'We worked out how to send coded messages from one electro-pulse to another. Mine got damaged and I've been trying to fix it ever since. I could send messages, but I couldn't receive any from him.'

'Why did he leave his electro-pulse behind in the IF ship?' Peri asked.

'I wanted Selene to know I'd received her messages,' Jaxx said softly.

'Enough of the sappy reunion!' Otto boomed. He grabbed Jaxx and pulled his hands behind his back. With his other arm he slipped a handcuff around Jaxx's wrist. 'We arrest him and finish the mission!'

'But my dad is innocent!' Selene protested. 'He's not a space pirate. Just give me a chance to prove to you that he isn't guilty of any crimes. Don't you want the truth? My dad didn't steal anything from the emperor!'

'Are you calling *my* dad a liar?' Diesel said. 'Jaxx is the liar here – and the thief. He stole the Heart of Mars. That's treason!'

Peri put his hand on the gunner's shoulder. 'Calm down, Diesel. Listen, if we want to recover the stolen gem, we need to hear Jaxx's side of the story.'

Jaxx cleared his throat. 'Someone stole my IF identity chip and used it to steal the jewel. I wasn't even on Mars when it happened. The IF wouldn't believe me. And what's worse, when they decided I was a space pirate, they started blaming me for other crimes.'

Peri studied Jaxx's face. He didn't look as though he was lying. 'So why did you come here?'

'I knew the only way to clear my name was to get the Heart of Mars back for the emperor, so I took an IF ship to go and find it. I think I've discovered where it is and I want to return it to prove my innocence.'

'It's true,' Selene chipped in. 'Peri, if we get the Heart of Mars back, we can catch the real pirates and still complete our mission. You have to trust me.'

'I've had enough!' Otto said. 'His innocence or guilt is not our problem! We should take him back!'

'My dad is telling the truth,' Selene pleaded. 'Who do you think taught me to be an engineer? A pirate or this man?'

Diesel let go of Jaxx. Diesel whispered in Peri's ear, 'I can't fail my father. We've got to do whatever it takes to find the Heart of Mars.'

Peri had one huge cosmic dilemma on his hands. Should he arrest Selene's dad or could he let him go? And if Jaxx didn't steal the Heart of Mars, then surely it was Peri's mission to find the real villain? Wasn't that what the IF creed was really about? And he'd promised to help Diesel recover the Heart of Mars too – didn't friendship come before orders?

'*Incoming message from General Pegg,*' the *Phoenix* announced as a monitor whirled from the control panel.

Instantly Selene shoved her dad to the deck. Otto threw himself behind the captain's chair. Peri pulled Diesel closer so that they blocked the view of the rest of the Bridge.

'What are you two up to?' General Pegg said as he appeared on the screen. 'I want a report now!'

'Umm, sir, we . . .'

'There is a problem with your Mission

Capsule,' Pegg continued. 'Why has it stopped sending data?'

Selene and her dad were huddled near Peri's feet. He glanced down and saw the Mission Capsule in Selene's hand. She smiled guiltily.

Peri looked up, knowing he couldn't betray his crew. 'I think that the capsule got damaged in a Zespa attack, sir.'

'What about Jaxx? Have you caught him yet?'

In the corner of his eye, Peri saw Jaxx trying to comfort Selene — as much as he could with his hands still cuffed behind his back. He certainly looked more like a concerned father than a sneaky villain. Peri had to trust Selene. If she said he was innocent, he believed her. It wasn't right to force them apart especially if they could find proof he wasn't really a pirate.

'Jaxx slipped away, sir, but we're on his trail!' Peri said.

The general sighed. 'Maybe I was right about the pair of you being too young to be Star Fighters,' he muttered. 'You have *one* more chance to complete your mission. If you fail again, you will return, and we will review whether you should be demoted back to cadet level. Terminate message.'

As the screen whirled back into the control panel, Otto stomped away from behind the captain's chair. 'You Earthlings are too soft! Meigwors don't give anyone a second chance!'

Selene jumped up. 'Thank you,' she said to Peri as she helped Jaxx up. 'I knew you would do the right thing.'

Peri looked at Diesel and knew he was thinking the same thing. They had taken a big risk for their friend, but they were going to prove General Pegg wrong. He and Diesel were not only old enough to be real Star Fighters, but they were the best Star Fighters in the entire Intergalactic Force. They would return the Heart of Mars to the emperor and bring the *real* pirates to justice!

Can they trust Jaxx? Who really stole the Heart of Mars?

Will Peri and Diesel survive an encounter with a terrifying Trojan Crab?

Find out! In . . .

Turn over to read Chapter 1

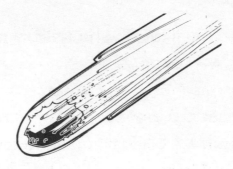

Chapter 1

'Wow!' Peri gasped. Through the 360-monitor, he could see a comet whooshing through outer space like an old-fashioned firework – the kind he had seen in *Did They Really Do That?*, a film about ancient Earth customs. The comet was going to miss the *Phoenix* by only a few hundred kilometres.

'We don't have time to admire the scenery, you voidoid,' Diesel said. 'Have you forgotten our mission? We have to recover the Heart of Mars.'

'And then hand over this criminal!' Otto

grunted. He flicked his long black tongue in Jaxx's direction. Their official Star Fighter mission was to capture the space pirate, but the emperor had also secretly commanded Diesel find and return the Heart of Mars.

Selene moved closer to Jaxx, her father. 'He's no pirate!'

'That's right, I'm not,' Jaxx said. His voice was mild, polite, friendly – the exact opposite of how Peri imagined a space pirate would sound.

Jaxx had escaped from prison and Peri and the crew of the *Phoenix* had finally chased him down in the rings of Saturn. They had rescued him from his stealth ship only a nanosecond before it blew up, and then arrested him. Only Selene's pleading had spared him from being turned in to the Intergalactic Force immediately.

Jaxx held out his hands. 'Perhaps you could take these handcuffs off me now?'

'We did agree to trust him,' Peri said, as he saw Otto eyeing Jaxx suspiciously.

'*I* didn't!' Otto boomed.

'Come on! He is our friend's dad,' Peri said. He touched a section of the wall and the Bits and Bobs drawer slid out. He pulled out the Universal Release Gun and pointed it at Jaxx's wrists. There was a sizzling sound and the handcuffs melted into a silvery goo that dripped on the floor of the Bridge.

'Hey!' Otto protested. 'Those handcuffs are my property!'

'*Were* your property,' Selene said with a grin.

'Thanks,' Jaxx said, shaking the goo from his hands.

'So, you say you know where the Heart of Mars is?' Diesel demanded.

The Heart of Mars was a priceless, glowing, orange orb of pure chrysolite from Mars, the size of a Meigwor's fist. It belonged to the Martian royal family. Diesel's father, the emperor, believed that all Martians would be cursed until the Heart of Mars was returned.

'I don't know for sure where it is,' Jaxx said. When Diesel's yellow eyes narrowed in disbelief, he quickly followed up with, 'But I do have a pretty good idea where to look.'

'Where, then?' Diesel pressed.

Jaxx pointed out of the 360-monitor. 'In that beautiful comet,' he said.

'That's the comet you plotted a course for, back on Haven?' Peri said.

Jaxx nodded. 'It's two years since the comet last passed through the Milky Way, and it's also two years since the Heart of Mars was stolen.'

Peri saw Diesel's fists clench. 'That doesn't prove anything!' Diesel shouted.

'I know,' Jaxx said. 'But I have strong reason to believe that . . . Well, just take it from me, the jewel is on that comet.'